CREEPERS

—Sydney V., 9, Murfreesboro

"These books are good stories that you will want to read.
Not too creepy, but scary enough!"

—Owen H., 10, Mansfield

"Creepers is an amazing series that keeps me turning pages
well past my bedtime (sorry mom)!"

—@pageturningpatrick, 11, Collingwood

"I wanted to keep reading, I didn't know what was going to happen
next! It was exciting and creepy all at the same time!"

—Avery H., 12, Hamilton

"Creepers is creepy, fun, and a bit mesmerizing!"

—Clara H., 10, Burlington

"The suspense kept me going! I can't wait to read the next book!!"

—Francesca N., 12, Jackson Heights

"The characters are very intriguing, and the ending
of the book was unpredictable."

—Abby, 11, Murfreesboro

"Those of the younger audience will get a cold shiver
down their back while reading this book,
as the same happened to me once or twice."

—Cameron, 13, Smyrna

"The content and ideas are
APPEALING, SPINE-CHILLING, GRUESOME
at times, extremely interesting, and sometimes even hilarious."

—Marla Conn, M.S. Ed., reading and literacy specialist
and educational consultant

The Gravedigger

by Edgar J. Hyde

Illustrations by Chloe Tyler

PAB-0608-0303 • ISBN: 978-1-4867-1879-5

Copyright ©2020 Flowerpot Press, a Division of Flowerpot Children's Press, Inc., Oakville, ON, Canada.

Printed and bound in the U.S.A.

Table of Contents

CHAPTER ONE

The New House

With every crack of lightning, Jamie's shadow was thrown against the wall. Lightning lit up his room for a split second before it was covered again with a blanket of darkness.

Outside, the icy night wind swirled around the graveyard, whistling through the gravestones and running down the old dirt track past the trees to the house at the bottom of the hill.

Inside, the house was in total darkness. The storm had knocked out the power a couple of hours ago, leaving Jamie, his younger sister, Paula, and his father, Andrew, fumbling around their new house in the pitch black, falling over unopened boxes and as usual in these circumstances, trying to scare the living daylights out of each other.

Jamie stood at the bottom of the long spiraling staircase that led upstairs to their bedrooms. He could hear someone moving around, squeaking the bare floorboards in his father's room.

It must be Dad, he thought. Paula's too light to make that kind of noise.

Slowly, he began to climb the stairs looking for Paula. He had an idea where his dad was, but Paula could be hiding anywhere waiting to pounce.

By now, the storm outside was getting worse. As Jamie crept past the window on the landing, another bolt of lightning lit up the staircase and the tall, dark figure that was creeping up the stairs behind him. Jamie continued to make his way up the stairs, completely unaware of the ghostly intruder. As he reached the top, he paused for a second, peering cautiously around the corner.

The door to his father's room was ajar but not

enough for Jamie to see inside. Knowing his family like he did, he knew that someone inside the room was waiting to jump out screaming and yelling.

Then Jamie heard breathing behind him. Quick as a flash he turned to see, but there was only darkness. The tall, dark figure that had floated behind him on the stairs was gone. The whole house was silent—eerily silent.

The creak of the bathroom door shattered the silence, and in a second, Jamie dashed into his little sister's room, leaving the door open a little so that he could still see out.

Then he saw it. The tall figure that followed him from downstairs passed through the bathroom door, turned, and made its way along the hall toward him.

It was a very tall man dressed in a long black cloak with swept back hair and bright white teeth that shone in the moonlight whenever he passed a window.

Before he reached his father's room, the door

opened and a familiar face stepped out from behind it. It was Paula.

The dark man glided along the hallway toward her. Paula, oblivious to what was over her shoulder, slipped out of the room and tiptoed her way down the hall.

Jamie stood watching everything from behind Paula's bedroom door, his heart beating faster and faster. The man came closer and closer, then suddenly Paula stopped.

Directly across from where Jamie stood was his own bedroom. Paula opened the door as quietly as she could, which was difficult because the door creaked with even the slightest movement, and stepped inside, closing the door behind her.

Jamie could hear his heart beating loud in his ears as he watched the dark figure hover outside the door with his long black cloak and dazzling white teeth. Jamie could tell he was a vampire.

The vampire waited a few moments before

disappearing through the door after Paula. Jamie stepped out from behind Paula's door into the hallway, took a deep breath, and prepared to charge.

"1,2,3," he counted, and as quick as his legs could carry him, he burst through the door!

"Aaaarrrgh!" he screamed as he ran straight into the middle of the room.

"Whoooaargh!!"

The roar of six separate voices came back at him. Jamie spun around. His dad was standing beside Paula, accompanied by a vampire, a mummy, a werewolf, and a man carrying his head under his arm. They were all laughing. Jamie took one look at them and burst out laughing himself.

Welcome to the Price family household. The Prices are no ordinary family. Ordinary families are usually scared of ghosts, but ghosts don't scare Jamie, his sister, or his father. In fact, there are certain ghosts who are more than friendly with the Prices. They're part of the family!

There's Count Vania, an unusual vampire who hates the sight of blood.

There's also Mummy, who has fascinated Jamie and his family late into the night with his tales of ancient Egypt and who amuses them even more by constantly tripping over his bandages.

Then there's Wolfie, the world's only vegetarian werewolf, who every time he catches a glimpse of himself in the mirror runs screaming from the room.

Last but not least, there's Lex Killon, an honorable old gentleman who was a passenger on the *Titanic* when it sank. Now Lex carries his head under his arm, accidentally spitting out salt water every time he opens his mouth.

Together, they are the only four ghosts that Jamie, his dad, and sister have not laid to rest. Not just because they are good friends, but because they help Jamie's dad earn a living writing horror novels.

It takes more than an ability to see ghosts to be able to write good horror stories. Jamie's dad

relies on the four friendly ghosts to give him all the information he needs about real ghosts and what makes them tick. That's what makes Andrew Price horror novels so good, because they're so real.

In fact, it's for that very reason that Jamie's dad bought their new house in the middle of the graveyard, much to Jamie and Paula's disapproval. Although they're not scared of ghosts, Jamie and Paula realized that as soon as their new classmates heard they lived in a graveyard, they would be regarded as either weird or spooky. But of course, their dad is the same as every dad—as soon as he gets something into his head, there's no getting it out again.

Whenever Jamie or Paula would tell him about their fears, he would simply smile, wink his eye and say, "Trust me," which always meant that nothing was going to go as planned.

"We nearly had you there, Jamie," said his father gleefully. By now everyone was giggling out loud.

Some, like Lex Killon, were giggling uncontrollably.

"No you didn't," replied Jamie. "I knew you were all in here. I was just trying to scare all of you first."

"Well you didn't scare me, that's for sure. I think you scared yourself more than anyone," said Paula.

Their dad agreed, "Yeah Jamie, you didn't scare me either. What about you, Count Vania?"

Count Vania floated into the middle of the room, still giggling.

"Well," he said, "there was no blood involved, so I wasn't the slightest bit scared."

"What about you, Mummy?" asked Andrew.

"No," came the muffled shout from Mummy. "It's the funniest thing I've seen in 2,000 years!"

Jamie was now getting a little frustrated. He knew he wasn't afraid but no one else in the room believed him.

"You never scared me," he said, trying to convince them, "and Mummy, if that's the funniest thing you've seen in 2,000 years, then you really should get out more often."

No sooner had the words left Jamie's mouth than the room was filled with laughter once again.

"Yeah, Mummy, you ought to get out more often!" shouted Wolfie.

"Oh really!" Mummy retorted. "Well why don't you take a look in the mirror?"

All around the room red faces were laughing hysterically.

I wish the power went out every night, thought Jamie. This is so much fun.

Outside, the wind continued to circle and swirl around the graveyard, and the rain continued to bounce hard off the windows.

Inside, Jamie and the others began making their way downstairs, their faces still red from laughing.

Suddenly, another crack of lightning lit up the graveyard to reveal a tall spooky figure standing under a tree at the end of the driveway.

It was Ebenezer Krim, the graveyard gardener.

He had been standing in the rain for some time watching the house, unable to see in because of the power outage. He stood there, not laughing or smiling, just staring.

CHAPTER TWO

Dominoes

With a loud thump, Jamie's dad dropped the book onto the desk, scattering the dust from beneath its pages in every direction. The noise it made echoed off the tall bookshelves and could be heard at the other end of the library.

"Shh," said the elderly man sitting at the desk across from them. It wasn't the first time the man had scolded Andrew. In fact, this was the fifth time Andrew had made a clatter. The last time it took an angry-looking librarian to get him to quiet down.

"Sorry," offered Andrew, looking around at the other tables to see if anyone else was getting annoyed with him before proceeding to pull his chair noisily across the wooden library floor.

Jamie and Paula tried hard not to laugh. The best Jamie could do was put his hand in front of his mouth, resulting in a loud pig-like snorting noise, which then resulted in another "Shh" from the man at the other table.

"You two be quiet. You're making too much noise," said Andrew.

"Us be quiet?" asked Paula incredulously. "You're the one who was told to quiet down!"

"Not true," replied her father. "I was just having an adult conversation with the librarian. That's what grown-ups do."

"Yeah that's right, Paula," added Jamie. "Dad was having a mature conversation with the lady."

"Thank you, Jamie," said his father, but before he could continue, Jamie interrupted him.

"And then she told him to shut up or get out!"

It doesn't take much to make Paula laugh and Jamie's latest remark was no exception, forcing her to giggle out loud and turn heads all over the library, once again bringing another "Shh" from the other table and yet another apology from her dad.

"When can we go home?" Jamie asked his dad, almost pleading with him.

"When I've found what I'm looking for," his dad replied sternly.

"Well what is it exactly that you're looking for?" asked Paula, trying very hard to sound helpful, but like Jamie, she was also desperate to get home.

"I'm looking for something suspicious about our new house, some record of ghastly encounters or details of a ghostly past," said her father, trying his best to involve them.

Now Paula was beginning to pay more attention. "Do you think there could be dead bodies buried at our house?"

"Gee, let me think..." answered Jamie. "We live in a house in the middle of a graveyard. You know, Paula, I think you could be right. I think if we look hard enough, we might find some dead bodies buried somewhere."

Paula hated it when Jamie made her look silly. It was something Jamie liked to do to his little sister at every opportunity.

"Jamie, stop poking fun at your sister," his father said. "Do something useful and start looking through those old newspaper clippings."

Jamie really didn't want to but in the end decided to help, if only to get home quicker.

The hours passed with Jamie, his father, and his sister searching through history books, flicking through newspaper clippings, and looking into the history of some of the people buried in the graveyard. But it was all for nothing. No horrific history, no ghastly past, no tales of ghosts or anything being haunted. Nothing.

Jamie's father slammed the final history book closed, forcing dust from beneath its cover and straight up his nose. He tried hard to contain a sneeze that somehow managed to squeeze between both his hands and out into the cold air of the library. Jamie and Paula were both sleeping with their heads on the desk, having given up on ever finding anything remotely spooky.

"Jamie, wake up," said his father, trying hard to shout a whisper.

Jamie raised his head from the desk. His hair was flat on one side of his head and his eyes barely opened as he whispered back.

"What is it? What did you find?"

"Nothing," replied his father. "But it's time to go home. They're closing the library for the night."

Jamie gave Paula a shake to wake her up, but Paula was so exhausted, she hardly felt a thing. Instead, she just rolled her head to the other side, making a loud grunting noise as Jamie continued to shake her and pull her hair. He eventually managed to wake her by slamming an encyclopedia onto the desk just inches from her head.

As they made their way to the exit, the librarian was already holding the door open, waiting for them to leave.

"Thank you," said Andrew as they passed through the doorway.

"You're welcome," replied the librarian, obviously glad to see Jamie and his family leaving. "Will you be back tomorrow?" she asked politely.

"No, no, I think we managed to look at everything we needed to," said Andrew, holding the door open for Jamie and Paula.

As they walked out into the cold night air, Jamie remembered that it had been daylight when they went into the library and how his father had claimed that it wouldn't take him long. Jamie looked at his watch and realized that was nearly six hours ago.

The house looked spooky enough during the day, but at night it looked even scarier. As Jamie's dad drove into the driveway, the wind seemed to get stronger and blow the leaves that had fallen from the trees high into the air. Paula zipped her jacket up and prepared to get out of the car and step into the freezing wind that was howling and whistling all around them.

Jamie looked up at the leaves that were blowing wildly into the dark night sky. Even the trees look evil he thought as he jumped out of the car and ran to the front door of the house.

The door creaked open, loud and slow, and one by one, Jamie, his sister, and his father emerged from behind it into the hallway of the house. As their dad pushed the door closed, some leaves blew inside and came to rest in front of Paula's feet.

"You two go upstairs and get into your pajamas. I'll make some hot chocolate," said their dad.

Jamie and Paula had just begun to climb the long spiraling staircase when they heard their father shout to them from the kitchen, "Jamie, Paula, come here for a second."

"What now?" muttered Paula, as she and Jamie turned and made their way back downstairs.

In the kitchen, Count Vania, Mummy, Wolfie, and Lex sat around the table. Jamie had seen this before. It meant that it was conference time. Either they had already done something or they were about to. It didn't take long to find out that it was the former.

"We didn't mean any harm," exclaimed Count Vania. "We were just having some fun."

"It's true," continued Lex Killon. "We were just playing a game. It was an accident."

"What exactly happened?" asked Andrew.

"Well, do you know how to play the game Leap Frog?" asked Wolfie.

"Yes," replied Jamie, Paula, and Andrew all at once.

"Well, it was kind of like that, only we weren't jumping over each other," said Wolfie.

"So what exactly were you jumping over?"

questioned Jamie.

"Gravestones," came a muffled answer from Mummy.

"Gravestones?" yelled Andrew. "What were you thinking?"

Wolfie started to get upset. "It was his fault!" he said pointing to Mummy. "We were all having fun until clumsy clogs tried it and fell over his bandages straight into one."

"Well, if you knocked one over I guess I'll have to be the one that picks it up," said Andrew angrily.

"Well, it wasn't just the one," Count Vania interrupted.

"So how many was it?" Jamie asked.

"I-I think the final figure was somewhere in the region of twenty-three," stuttered Lex.

"How on earth did you manage to knock over twenty-three gravestones?" yelled Andrew.

"It was a bit like when you put lots of dominoes close together in a line and then push one over," muttered Mummy sheepishly.

"Did anyone see you?" Paula asked.

The four of them looked at each other with blank expressions. The truth was none of them noticed if they were being watched, so they couldn't be sure.

"I think the four of you should keep a VERY low profile for the next couple of days," bellowed Andrew. "Don't you?"

"Yes," came their murmured halfhearted replies.

"And I think you should start right now," said Andrew.

One by one, they stood up from the table and disappeared through the wall, apologizing as they went.

Jamie looked at Paula.

"It's been a long day," he said.

"Yep," Paula replied, "and I've got a funny feeling we haven't heard the last of this."

CHAPTER THREE

Accused

The events of the previous night did not pass unnoticed the next day. Everyone in the house seemed to be on edge, as though they were expecting something to happen.

The four culprits hadn't shown their faces around the house, obviously keeping a low profile as requested.

Jamie was in the living room watching TV and his dad was in the kitchen standing over a sink full of dirty breakfast dishes. He seemed a million miles away as he stood gazing out the window with a strange look on his face.

By the sound of things, Paula was upstairs

practicing her dance routines. The loud banging and thumping of her dancing around her room could be heard in every room downstairs.

Jamie stood up and walked to the window. Outside it was a gray day with no real hint of sunshine breaking through the dark clouds that seemed to hang over the graveyard. Every time Jamie looked out the window, he got the feeling that somewhere out among the moss-covered headstones and dark overhanging trees, someone was watching him.

Great, thought Jamie, even during the day, this place gives me the creeps. As he turned and walked away from the window, the sound of the doorbell echoed throughout the house. Even Paula heard it over the thumping of her music.

That's weird, thought Jamie. To get to the front door you have to walk past the window, and I was just standing there and never saw anyone come through the gate.

"Could someone get the door, please?" yelled Andrew from the kitchen.

"I'll get it," Paula shouted as she came running down the stairs two at a time.

Jamie and Paula liked to compete with each other at everything. No matter how silly the task was, one of them had to be the quickest or the smartest or the funniest, just to be better than the other one.

However, this time, Paula was certainly going to win the race to answer the door because Jamie remained still, not sure of what might be standing on the other side of the door.

Paula jumped down the last few stairs and reached the door.

"I got here first," she said, turning to make sure Jamie heard her.

Jamie remained in the living room as Paula heaved open the large wooden front door. A tall, thin man was standing in the doorway. Paula's head was directly in line with the man's waist, and slowly

her eyes started to climb upward.

The man was wearing chunky black boots that were caked with mud. His black pants were patched at the knee and tucked inside his boots. From what she could see of his sweater, it was dirty and frayed at the bottom, but it was difficult to see because the man was wearing a long, black coat that reached the top of his knees and smelled awful. As Paula looked up at the stranger's face, it was difficult to see it because he was wearing a black hat that cast a shadow over his face.

The man bent down toward Paula, coming close to her face, and she saw that he had very pale skin, almost ghostly, and a thin, pointy nose with big nostrils.

Paula felt a shiver run down her spine.

"Is your father here?" he asked Paula, so close to her face she could feel his warm breath on her cheeks, smell his bad breath in her nose, and see the yellow stains on his teeth.

"Who's at the door?" yelled Andrew from the kitchen.

"It's someone for you, Dad," Paula replied, taking a step back from the stranger.

Jamie walked to the front door. At the same time, his father walked from the kitchen, drying his hands on a towel before handing it to Jamie to hold for him.

"Allow me to introduce myself," said the man to Andrew. "My name is Ebenezer Krim."

Paula looked at Jamie. It was one of the few occasions that Jamie could remember seeing fear in her face.

"Nice to meet you. I'm Andrew Price," said Andrew politely.

"I'm the gardener for the graveyard," Mr. Krim continued.

"How did you reach the front door?" interrupted Jamie.

"I walked straight up the path and past the

window," Mr. Krim said.

"You couldn't have," Jamie replied.

"Didn't you see me?" Mr. Krim replied. "I saw you."

The thought that this strange-looking man had been watching Jamie without him knowing made Jamie's blood run cold.

"Would you like to come in for a cup of coffee?" asked Andrew.

Jamie looked at his dad in disbelief. What on earth was he doing inviting this man into their home?

"I'd love a coffee," Mr. Krim replied.

"Jamie, run into the kitchen and get some coffee for Mr. Krim," said his father.

Ebenezer Krim stepped inside the hallway, stamping his feet on the rug and knocking off large clumps of dried mud, as Jamie's dad closed the door behind him with a loud thud.

As Mr. Krim made his way into the sitting room,

Jamie pulled his dad back by the arm.

"Dad, I don't know what it is about that man, but something isn't right," he whispered.

His father seemed annoyed with him. "Be careful," he said. "Mr. Krim might hear you."

"Why did you invite him in?" Jamie asked.

"Well, I don't know if you're seeing something I'm not, but the man seems perfectly nice to me," his father replied.

"But he's lying! He never passed by the window."

Jamie started to get very frustrated with his father. To him it was so obvious that Mr. Krim was a very strange man.

"Jamie, if he didn't pass you at the window, how else could he have walked up to the front door?" his father asked.

"I don't know," said Jamie. "That's what's so spooky about him."

"I've heard enough," said his father sternly. "There's nothing wrong with Mr. Krim. You hardly even know the man."

"But…" said Jamie, trying to interrupt.

"No buts," continued his father. "Go and pour Mr. Krim a cup of coffee like I asked. Then come and join the rest of us in the sitting room."

Jamie didn't argue. He knew his dad couldn't be talked into agreeing with him. Instead, Jamie headed off to the kitchen to do what his father had asked.

A few minutes later, Jamie emerged from the kitchen carrying a tray with coffee for his dad and Mr. Krim and hot chocolate for him and Paula. As he walked into the living room, he could see his father was sitting on one chair and Paula on the other.

Great, he thought. Now I'll have to sit beside Mr. Krim on the couch.

Jamie set the tray down on the table and chose the seat on the other end of the couch from Mr. Krim.

As his dad handed Mr. Krim his coffee, Mr. Krim

began to speak.

"You know, some people around here say things about me that aren't really true. They like to spread rumors."

"Really?" asked Andrew.

"Yes," continued Mr. Krim, "they only say these things because they don't really know me. It's mainly the kids. They call me spooky or weird."

"I can't imagine why," said Jamie, trying hard to sound sincere when he really didn't want to.

His dad gave him a look that told him to be quiet. Ebenezer Krim seemed to not notice and continued.

"A lot of the time, the kids say things to hide their own guilt."

"What do you mean?" asked Andrew.

"Well, sometimes they'll do something they shouldn't have—something bad—then tell lies about me so that I get the blame and they get out of trouble."

"That's terrible," replied Andrew.

"I know, which brings me to the reason I'm visiting you. Last night we had a bit of trouble in the graveyard."

Jamie and Paula both looked at each other, dreading what Mr. Krim was going to say next.

"Some headstones were knocked over," he continued.

"How many?" asked Andrew, trying hard to act as if he didn't know.

"There were twenty-three in total," replied Mr. Krim. "Where exactly were your kids last night, Mr. Price?" he asked suspiciously.

"My kids?" said Andrew, a little confused by the question. "Jamie and Paula were at the library with me all night."

"And what time did you get home?" Mr. Krim continued, looking at Jamie and Paula with his piercing eyes.

"I really don't like what you are trying to say

Mr. Krim," said Andrew.

"Neither do I," continued Jamie.

Paula remained silent.

"My kids were with me all night," Andrew went on, "and at no time did they leave my sight. So it wasn't them that pushed the headstones over."

Ebenezer Krim didn't say anything. There was a long silence that made Jamie, Andrew, and Paula very uncomfortable. Mr. Krim just sat staring at everyone, his eyes slowly moving from Andrew to Paula to Jamie. Eventually he turned his gaze back to Paula.

"It was you, wasn't it?" he yelled.

Paula looked frightened as she sat on the chair not saying anything.

"I think you should leave," shouted Andrew to Mr. Krim. "We've all heard enough."

Mr. Krim appeared not to hear him. His eyes and attention were fixed on Paula.

"You did it for fun, didn't you?" he said to her.

"No I didn't," replied Paula. "And anyway, it was an accident."

Jamie winced.

"Ah-ha!" Mr. Krim yelled triumphantly. "So you did do it."

Paula started to get very angry.

Jamie shouted at Mr. Krim, "Leave her alone." But again, Mr. Krim ignored him.

"I told you to leave," said Andrew.

"Why did you do it?" Mr. Krim snarled at Paula.

"I told you, I didn't," she yelled back.

"Well who was it then? Your brother?"

Paula couldn't take anymore.

"No it wasn't Jamie either. It was the ghosts," she shouted at Mr. Krim.

The room fell into silence.

"Ghosts?" Mr. Krim said with a smirk on his face.

"Are you trying to tell me evil ghosts knocked the headstones over?"

"They're not bad ghosts. They're good ghosts, and

they're our friends."

"Paula, be quiet!" Jamie yelled at her.

Mr. Krim looked around the room. The look on their faces made him believe that Paula was telling the truth.

"I told you to leave, Mr. Krim," Andrew said.

Ebenezer Krim did not reply. He stood up, put his cup on the table, and made his way to the front door. As he reached the front door, he turned to Jamie's father.

"Believe me when I say this, Mr. Price, this is not the last you will hear from me," he said before slamming the door closed behind him.

Everyone in the living room sat in silence, thinking about what had just happened. Now Ebenezer Krim knew their secret.

Andrew looked at both Jamie and Paula and said, "We all need to talk. I think this is just the beginning of our trouble with Mr. Krim."

CHAPTER FOUR

Kitchen Table Conference

"This is not good," said Count Vania.

There were more than a few concerned faces around the kitchen table, and they weren't all human.

Jamie's father had just filled them in on what happened the day before when Ebenezer Krim paid them a visit, and now the ghosts were beginning to realize just how costly their game of Headstone Leap Frog might prove to be.

As always, when something important needed to be discussed, everyone would gather around the kitchen table.

"This is all my fault," muttered Mummy through

a face full of bandages.

"No it isn't," said Jamie. "It's no one's fault. Accidents happen."

"Yeah, but if I hadn't let the cat out of the bag, we wouldn't be in this mess," whined Paula.

Andrew put a comforting arm around her.

"Jamie's right, Paula," he said. "No one's to blame for any of this. These things happen. We've just got to figure out a way to get out of this."

Everyone agreed.

"I think the best plan of action would be to simply seek out this Krim chap and apologize," said Lex Killon.

"I think it's too late for that," Jamie replied. "Mr. Krim seemed really angry when he left."

Andrew agreed.

"Yeah, I think Ebenezer Krim wants everyone to know that he wasn't to blame for the headstones being knocked over."

"So what do we do then?" asked Wolfie.

"I think the only thing we can do is wait and see what happens," replied Andrew. "Mr. Krim said it wouldn't be the last we would hear from him. He's found out some information about us, so it's up to him now to decide what he wants to do with it."

Paula got up from the table and started pacing the floor. Something was obviously on her mind.

"What's wrong, Paula?" asked Jamie.

"I'm just thinking," she replied. "What if the other kids in my class find out that we hang out with ghosts? They won't want to talk to me. They'll all think that I'm creepy."

"They probably think that already," said Jamie.

"That's not funny," Paula retorted.

Sometimes Jamie would make jokes at the wrong time, and this was the wrong time.

"There's no point in worrying about that, Paula," Andrew said. "We don't know what's going to happen."

"Why don't I go to Mr. Krim's house and scare

the living daylights out of him?" suggested Wolfie.

"Because there might be mirrors in his house and you'll end up more scared than him," replied Count Vania.

"Well, we've got to do something," said Jamie. "We can't just sit here and wait for him to go and tell the police or something."

"I don't think anyone would believe him anyway," muttered Mummy.

Lex Killon tried to say something, but as soon as he opened his mouth, some salt water squirted out straight into Andrew's coffee mug.

"Oh, I'm frightfully sorry," he said.

Jamie's dad emptied the cup down the sink and smiled. "Forget about it," he said.

"I wouldn't be so sure that no one will believe him," added Lex Killon. "When you think about it, it does sound a bit odd."

"What do you mean?" asked Andrew.

"Well, look at it the way other people will look at

it. You bought a house in the middle of a graveyard. It's quite a spooky thing to do."

The others wanted to disagree but knew that Lex was right.

"And the head of the family writes horror novels for a living, " continued Lex.

For the first time since they all sat down, the kitchen was silent. Lex had made everyone realize that Mr. Krim could make things really difficult for them in town.

"I think the best thing would be for the four of us to find somewhere else to hang around," said Count Vania. His words seemed very loud in the silence of the kitchen, even though he rarely raised his voice above a whisper.

"I think you're right," agreed Wolfie. "If we go now, things might not be so bad with Mr. Krim."

"No!" shouted Jamie in a panic. "We don't want you to go. We want you to stay here with us."

Jamie hardly ever lost his cool. He wasn't the type

that scared easily or panicked. In fact, it took an awful lot to scare Jamie, but the look on his face told everyone at the table that he was scared his ghost friends would leave him for good.

"I'm with Jamie on this one," added Andrew. "We've got to stick together. You guys are a part of our family, so we want you to stay."

"Will you stay?" Paula asked.

Slowly, one by one, Count Vania, Wolfie, Mummy, and Lex Killon nodded their heads. Although they never said it, Jamie could tell they were glad they could stay.

"We have to tread very carefully for the next few days," said Andrew. "So here's what we have to do..."

Jamie sat forward at the table, as did everyone else, waiting to hear what his father had to say.

"For the time being, there are to be no more hauntings. Wolfie, if you want a veggie burger, we'll get it for you. Don't go near the store."

"No problem," replied Wolfie.

Andrew continued, "Mummy, you'll have to stay away from the Ancient Egyptian Museum."

"But I go there to visit my cousins," he protested.

"I know," replied Andrew, "but we can't risk anyone catching a glimpse of any of you. The same goes for you, Count Vania and Lex."

Count Vania nodded his head, while Lex clasped his head between both his hands, nodded, and then placed his head back on the table.

As Jamie's dad continued with his instructions to the rest of the family, Ebenezer Krim stood outside watching them.

Long after Count Vania and the rest of the ghosts had gone, Ebenezer still stood outside the house in the dark. He hadn't moved once; he just stood there in the pouring rain, staring into the house.

It wasn't until Andrew's bedroom light went off that Mr. Krim turned and walked away. As he trudged through the mud, he turned and whispered, "Tomorrow I'm going to make you pay. I'm going to make you all pay."

CHAPTER FIVE

The Reporter

The office door to the *Blackhearth Gazette* was thrown open with force, banging the door of the nearby filing cabinet, as the unmistakable figure of Ebenezer Krim marched in with his muddy boots and pressed the buzzer on the desk.

His eyes scanned every inch of the office, past the old newspaper clippings that were framed on the wall, the pile of newspapers that were tied together on the table, the computers, the printers, the telephones, and eventually stopped on a framed headline that read "Famous Horror Writer Moves to Blackhearth." It was an article from the previous week's newspaper about Andrew Price.

Ebenezer's face began to change as he read every word of the article. He could feel the rage inside him ready to erupt. His eyes got visibly smaller the angrier he became.

"Can I help you?" said the voice from the other side of the counter.

Ebenezer lifted his evil face to look at the man. He could tell the man was obviously afraid of him.

"I'd like to give you some information for a story. My name is Ebenezer Krim."

"I know who you are," said the other man. "My name is Mike Philips. I'm one of the reporters here."

Although Mr. Philips had never met or spoken to Ebenezer Krim before, he still knew exactly who he was. There wasn't one person in the whole town of Blackhearth who didn't know who Ebenezer Krim was.

"Well if you're a reporter, then you're just who I'm looking for," Ebenezer replied. "I just read the article in last week's paper about Mr. Price."

"Yes, that was a good story for us. It's not every day a famous writer and his family move to Blackhearth," Mr. Philips interrupted.

Ebenezer Krim said nothing. Instead, he tilted his head back so that his eyes were peering at Mr. Philips from under his hat. He stared down his nose at him and finally said, "Now hear this..."

The evil look on his face and the way in which he said it sent a shiver down Mr. Philips's spine.

"Mr. Andrew Price and the rest of his family aren't as nice as everyone seems to think," Mr. Krim continued.

"Oh really?" replied Mike Philips, trying hard to appear calm. "What exactly are they then?"

Ebenezer looked around the office, eventually stopping once again on the article about Andrew Price.

"What if I could give you a story that would have everyone in Blackhearth demanding the Price family be thrown out?"

"I would say tell me more," said Mr. Philips. By now his fear was gone and was replaced with curiosity.

"I'll tell you what Andrew Price and his two brats are—they're devil worshipers," said Ebenezer Krim. "They talk to the evil spirits of dead people."

Mr. Philips stood back from the desk, his face appeared disappointed and a little annoyed by what Ebenezer had just told him.

"Let me get this straight," he said. "You're telling me that a respected writer and his family, who have just moved into the house in the graveyard that you wanted to buy, talk to ghosts? Well how exactly do they do that, Mr. Krim?" he asked.

"I don't know," replied Ebenezer Krim. "They must have strange powers or something."

"Oh, this just gets better. Not only do they talk to ghosts, but they're also psychic," said Mr. Philips, making fun of Mr. Krim.

Ebenezer leaned across the desk, the pale white

skin of his face so close to Mike Philips that he could see his own reflection in Ebenezer's eyes.

"I hope you're not making fun of me," said Ebenezer through gritted teeth.

"N-N-No," said Mr. Philips, nervously stammering over his words. "I just don't think that too many people will believe your story. I mean, do you have any proof?"

Ebenezer stepped back from the desk.

"Proof?" he said. "What kind of proof?"

"Well, anything that might back up your story," Mr. Philips replied, "like photographs or a taped conversation or something. How exactly did you find all of this out?"

Ebenezer thought for a second before replying.

"Did you hear about the incident the other night with the headstones?" he asked.

"Yes," said Mike Philips.

"Well, it was the evil spirits the Price family are friends with. They were responsible."

"Again, Mr. Krim, do you have any proof?" questioned Mr. Philips.

"Of course I do!" yelled Ebenezer Krim who was getting irritated by the reporter across the desk from him. "The youngest one—the girl—she told me in front of the other two."

Mike Philips took a step back and a deep breath. He didn't like the idea of telling Ebenezer Krim that his proof wasn't actually proof.

"Think of it like this, Mr. Krim," he began, "there are a lot of people in this town that find you very strange. Some people even call you spooky."

Ebenezer's nostrils began to flare with rage.

"I'm not saying I do," said Mr. Philips, trying to calm him down slightly, "but some people do. Now if I was to print a story in the paper that called Mr. Price and his family devil worshipers just because you say they are, no one is going to believe it."

"Let's find out," announced Ebenezer Krim.

"I can't. I need more proof than the person who

wanted to buy their house saying he was told so by an eight-year-old girl."

"There's the headstone incident," said Ebenezer.

"Most people in this town already think that you knocked the headstones over," replied Mr. Philips.

Ebenezer slowly leaned over the desk to Mike Philips, beads of sweat running down his face.

"Are you telling me," Ebenezer asked slowly, "that you won't print the story?"

"I'm telling you that I can't," replied Mr. Philips in a nervous, croaky voice.

"Well if you won't help me get rid of these people, I'll have to do it myself," said Ebenezer Krim. He gave Mike Philips a long, evil stare before turning and walking out of the office.

As Ebenezer left, Mr. Philips sat down on a chair and gave a loud sigh. He hoped that this was the last he would ever hear from Ebenezer Krim.

"Good luck, Mr. Price," he whispered. "You're going to need it."

CHAPTER SIX

Run

It felt like the first time that Andrew had seen the sun since they moved into their new house. He'd spent all morning working on his new book and decided it was time for a break.

As he wandered out into his backyard, he glanced at the sky above him. It was clear blue without a cloud in sight.

It's about time, he thought. We've had nothing but dark clouds, rain, thunder, and lightning every day for the past week.

The ghosts hadn't showed up all day. As Andrew sipped his cup of coffee, he hoped that they were keeping out of trouble, which is difficult for four friendly ghosts with a lot of spare time on their hands.

Andrew reclined in the lounge chair, picked up his newspaper, and relaxed in the warm morning sunshine. Within minutes he had dozed off.

Jamie used to joke about his father's ability to sleep at any time of the day. Even if he'd just woken up from a good night's sleep, he could fall asleep again within minutes.

"It's a dad thing," Paula says. "If he didn't fall asleep all the time, he wouldn't be a normal dad."

Of course Jamie would argue that he has never been a normal dad.

"Aaaaarrrggh!"

A scream seemed to pierce Andrew, waking him up in an instant. As he jumped to his feet, still half asleep, he spun around in a desperate attempt to figure out where the scream had come from. The scream was unmistakable—it was Wolfie.

It wasn't just the scream that woke him up but

a deep rumbling sound that seemed to be getting louder. As Andrew looked up, he could see what was making the loud rumbling.

The blue skies had turned gray, and there, racing toward him, was a large black cloud that rolled across the sky, getting closer and closer and louder and louder, and with it came the terrified screams of Wolfie, Count Vania, Mummy, and Lex Killon.

From out of nowhere, Count Vania flew through the wall and across the backyard to Andrew.

"He's coming after us!" he screamed.

"Who's coming after you?" Andrew asked.

Before he could answer, Lex Killon came screaming through the wall closely followed by Mummy. As they ran across the yard, Lex dropped his head and Mummy fell over his bandages.

"He's right behind us!" shouted Lex.

"Get in the house!" yelled Mummy.

"What's going on?" asked Andrew again.

"There's no time to explain," said Count Vania.

"Just get inside quickly."

As they ran toward the back door that led into the kitchen, Wolfie's screaming could be heard in the distance.

"Run, Wolfie, run!" yelled Lex Killon, as Andrew followed the ghosts inside.

Andrew slammed the door closed and bolted it.

"What about Wolfie?" asked Mummy. "How will he get in?"

"The same way he always does. He'll run straight through it," answered Andrew, running to the window.

"Tell me the truth right now," he continued. "What have you done and who is chasing you?"

"We haven't done anything," shouted Count Vania. "It's Ebenezer Krim! He's after us."

"He has a big machine and he's trying to suck us into it," said Mummy.

Just then, across the grass, they could see Wolfie. By now the clouds that raced across the sky were

above the house. As Wolfie sprinted for the door, Andrew noticed that something behind the wall was sucking everything toward it. The trees in the yard were bent backwards by the suction of the powerful vacuum, their leaves getting ripped off the branches. And Wolfie was being pulled back across the grass toward whatever it was.

"Keep running, Wolfie!" screamed Andrew. "Keep running!"

It was as though Wolfie was running and getting nowhere, but slowly he made it to the door. From inside the kitchen the rest of them could see Wolfie's hands appearing through the door first followed by his head.

Mummy ran to him, grabbed him by the ears, and yanked him inside, forcing both of them to fall to the floor.

Andrew turned and looked back out the window. Things were calming down. The trees had returned to their normal shape and only a few things were being sucked through the air and down behind the wall.

Then suddenly there was silence.

Andrew could hear his own breathing loud in his ears. He turned and looked at the others. By now, Wolfie was on his feet and stood with his back to the door, puffing and panting.

Outside, the daylight was slowly leaving, being replaced by darkness. It looked as though someone was dimming the lights.

A familiar evil face appeared above the wall. It was Ebenezer Krim. His long pale face looked even more menacing than it did before as he climbed to the top of the wall, hoisting a long black machine up beside him.

The machine itself looked no more dangerous than a normal vacuum, except it had a few more lights and made a louder noise. Andrew guessed that this was the machine Ebenezer was using to suck everything up.

"What happened out there?" asked Andrew, turning to the rest of them.

"We were on our way here," replied Count Vania, "when all of a sudden he appeared before us, waving that machine and shouting how he was going to get us."

"And you weren't causing any trouble?" asked Andrew.

"No, we were minding our own business," replied Wolfie.

"Do you think he saw you, the same way Jamie, Paula, and I can?"

"No, he's just the same as other humans," replied Count Vania. "He can only see us for short periods of time."

"I know you're in there!" came a shout from the darkness outside. Ebenezer Krim was sitting on top of the wall holding his machine.

"How do you like my little homemade ghost killer?" he asked, patting the machine. "Quite powerful, isn't it?" he laughed. Even his laugh sounded evil, like a witch's deep cackle.

"That man scares me," said Mummy.

Andrew looked around the kitchen at the others. They were in agreement with Mummy. It seemed the only person who wasn't afraid of Ebenezer Krim was Andrew.

"What do you want, Mr. Krim?" shouted Andrew through the window.

"It's quite simple," he replied. "I would like all of the ghosts to come out here, one by one."

"Why do you want them to come out?" asked Andrew. "Do you want to talk to them?"

"No, Mr. Price," Mr. Krim replied. "I don't want to talk to them. I want to destroy them!"

Wolfie, Count Vania, Mummy, and Lex Killon all looked at each other. No one said anything, but they were all thinking the same thing, and they couldn't hide it. They were terrified.

"In that case, Mr. Krim, they won't be coming

out," yelled Andrew.

Mr. Krim didn't seem bothered.

"That's okay," he replied. "I can wait. I'll wait all night if I have to."

Andrew turned to the others and said, "Don't panic, he's bluffing. He'll be gone in a couple of hours."

Lex Killon went to speak, but as always, he only managed to spit some salt water onto the floor.

"Sorry," he murmured. "I'm not so sure myself. Mr. Ebenezer Krim seems a very determined sort of chap."

"Well," replied Andrew, "we'll just have to stay in here until he decides to leave."

"How long do you think that will take?"asked Mummy.

"As long as it takes," Andrew answered.

It was the daylight on Jamie's face that eventually woke him. He turned his sleepy head around the kitchen to see his father asleep on the chair, Paula asleep on the table, and the ghosts asleep anywhere there was a space.

Jamie and Paula had arrived home from school the previous day to find themselves in the middle of a standoff between everyone in their house and Ebenezer Krim.

Jamie got up from the table and walked to the window, just in time to see Ebenezer Krim climb down from the wall and drag his machine away across the grass behind him and up the hill.

As he reached the top of the hill, he turned and stared back at Jamie. Although it was only for a few seconds, to Jamie it felt like hours. Even though he was far away, Jamie could still make out his evil grin as he turned and walked over the hill.

No doubt we'll be seeing you again, Mr. Krim, thought Jamie.

CHAPTER SEVEN

The Gravedigger

Ebenezer Krim didn't know he was being watched.

As he sat in his own dirty living room covered in dust and flooded with mice scrambling across the floor, running into every little nook and cranny in the walls, he was completely unaware that sitting across the table from him was a ghost.

It wasn't Count Vania, or Mummy, or Lex Killon, or Wolfie, this was a ghost that Ebenezer hadn't seen before and couldn't see now.

The ghost had long, skinny white fingers, a long, thin body, and a wrinkly, scarred face with black holes where his eyes should be.

Ebenezer was polishing his machine, getting ready to destroy some ghosts like he had tried to the previous night, when he heard some scratching noises coming from the other side of the table. He stopped what he was doing immediately and listened.

The ghost that he couldn't see got up from the chair across from him and floated across the table toward him, stopping inches from his face.

Ebenezer Krim knew that something was there, but he wasn't sure what exactly.

Then he heard it. The scratching began again. The ghost was dragging his long fingernails across the table in front of him, marking the wood.

Ebenezer looked down at the long, thin scratches that were appearing on his table and knew that somewhere in front of him was a ghost.

One yank by Ebenezer on the chain and his sucking machine roared to life. He kicked back his chair, swung the tube toward the ghost in front of him, and flipped the switch.

Broken plates and cups started flying around the room, along with pictures, ornaments, and anything that wasn't screwed down. It was all sucked into the air and down the long, black tube Ebenezer held in his hand.

"Time to die, Mr. Ghosty!" he screamed at the top of his lungs, as most of his living room began to disappear inside the machine. Even after he switched it off, it took a couple of minutes for the room to settle.

Ebenezer stood in the middle of the room, panting and wheezing as sweat dripped off the end of his pointy nose.

His face had a horrible grin on it. This was the first time Ebenezer had used the machine on a ghost, and he was sure it had worked.

Then he heard the same scratching noise he heard before, but this time it was behind him.

Now Ebenezer Krim was angry.

"I'm going to rip you into little pieces and kill you!" he screamed as he spun the machine around and once again flipped the switch.

Before the machine had a chance to start up, Ebenezer was flung across the room, banging off the wall and falling on the floor.

He staggered to his feet.

"Where are you?" he yelled.

In a flash, the ghost appeared in front of him, frightening him so much that he staggered back and fell down.

"Don't even think about using that machine again," the ghost said to him.

"Who are you?" asked Ebenezer.

"I'm an old employee of this graveyard," the ghost replied. "I used to be the gravedigger."

Ebenezer got to his feet again.

"What do you want from me?" he asked.

"I want you to help me get rid of the Prices," the gravedigger replied.

Ebenezer sat down, not taking his eyes off the ghost for a second. Although he hated ghosts, he was beginning to hate Jamie and his family even more.

"Go on," said Mr. Krim. Now he was curious to hear what the ghost had to say.

"One thing I noticed yesterday," began the gravedigger, "was how much you managed to scare the Price family. I thought nothing could scare that family. Certainly not ghosts!"

"Were you there yesterday?" asked Ebenezer. "Because I never saw you."

"You never saw me because I never wanted you or the Prices to see me," continued the gravedigger.

"But the Prices can see all ghosts," said Ebenezer.

"I know," said the gravedigger. "They would have been able to see me had I not learned how to hide. You only see me if I want you to see me."

"Well what about the ghosts? Surely they can see you," Ebenezer said.

"Yes, they can see me," he replied, "but I can also

turn myself into other ghosts. So I can appear as one of the ghost friends and no one would know the difference."

Ebenezer sat for a few seconds thinking about what the gravedigger had just said, and then he asked, "Why do you want to get rid of the Price family?"

The gravedigger floated toward Ebenezer Krim.

"The reason I want to get rid of them," he began, "is because ever since they moved into that house, they've made my afterlife miserable. Things used to be peaceful before they came."

Ebenezer Krim nodded in agreement. At last he had someone who thought like him on his side.

"If you want to get rid of those four ghosts that live with the Prices, don't waste your time with silly machines. All you have to do is get rid of the Prices. The ghosts will follow them anywhere," said the gravedigger.

"But," Ebenezer interrupted, "don't the Prices

look for evil spirits, like you, and try to put them to rest?"

"Let me worry about that," replied the gravedigger. "So, what do you say? Are you going to help me get rid of them?"

Ebenezer looked at him with his evil eyes and said, "What if I don't help you?"

The gravedigger moved closer to Ebenezer, right up to his face, and said, "If you don't help me, I'll get rid of you, too."

For the first time in his life, Ebenezer Krim felt scared.

"How are we going to get rid of them?" he asked.

"It's quite simple, we'll either scare them out or we'll throw them out," said the gravedigger.

As Ebenezer watched the gravedigger laugh at the thought of it, he knew that this was the beginning of very horrible things to come.

CHAPTER EIGHT

An Appearance

"Jamie Price, will you please pay attention and stop staring out the window?" yelled Jamie's teacher for the fourth time that morning.

Jamie always did have trouble concentrating in school, and biology class wasn't any exception.

Jamie turned to face his teacher and murmured, "Sorry."

His teacher accepted his apology and turned back to the rest of the class.

Jamie turned back to the window and looked at the students in the class outside.

Jamie was more than a little spooked by what had happened over the past couple of days. Ghosts he could handle, but an evil person like Mr. Krim was a different story.

Paula was the same. She told Jamie on the way to school that morning that she had a feeling something bad was going to happen. Jamie told her it was just her imagination, but what he didn't tell her was that he had the same feeling.

As Jamie watched the students outside, a tall, dark figure on the opposite end of the soccer field caught his eye. As soon as Jamie realized who it was, his blood ran cold. It was Ebenezer Krim.

Ebenezer started walking toward Jamie, his evil stare fixed on him. Jamie's heart started to beat faster. He could feel it beating hard inside his chest. He turned to look at his teacher, but she had her back to him and was writing on the board.

Jamie looked back at Ebenezer Krim. He was so close that Jamie could see the evil grin on his face.

"Jamie Price, for the last time, will you please pay attention!" yelled his teacher at him.

"Please, there's a man looking at me through the window. It's Ebenezer Krim."

The rest of Jamie's class gasped out loud. Every other kid in his class knew who Ebenezer Krim was and so did his teacher. She hurried toward Jamie's desk and stopped when she was beside him.

"Where is he, Jamie?" she asked.

Jamie turned back to the window, but Ebenezer was gone.

"He was just there," said Jamie, pointing to where Mr. Krim had been.

"Are you playing a prank, Jamie?" asked his teacher.

"No, it's the truth," said Jamie, pleading his innocence. His teacher gave him a look of disbelief before walking back to the front the classroom.

Jamie turned and looked back out the window to where he had seen Ebenezer Krim. He was still nowhere to be seen. He was definitely there, Jamie thought. I definitely saw his face.

Meanwhile, back at the house, Andrew was busy putting up some shelves in their living room. It had been a quiet morning for him with none of the other ghosts around. They were too busy keeping out of the way in case they saw Ebenezer Krim and his ghost-sucking machine.

"Hello there," said a voice behind him. He turned around to see Count Vania floating in the middle of the room.

"Hi, Count Vania, where is the rest of the gang hanging out this morning?" he asked.

"I'm not really sure," replied the count, looking in the opposite direction.

That's strange, thought Jamie's father, they normally always know where the others are.

"I'd like to have a word with you, if I could," said Count Vania.

"Sure you can," replied Andrew. "What would you like to talk about?"

"I'd like to talk about moving," said Count Vania. "I was just wondering if we might be moving again soon."

Andrew put down his hammer and turned around to face the count.

"Why?"

"To tell you the truth, I don't like it here," said the count. "I think everyone would be a lot happier if we just moved."

"This is a little out of character for you," replied Andrew. "Normally you settle in quite easily whenever we move."

Count Vania turned his back on Andrew. "I just don't like this house. Ever since we moved in, we've had nothing but trouble."

"Does this have anything to do with Ebenezer Krim?" asked Andrew.

"The other day, I really thought he was going to hurt me," replied the count.

Jamie's father could see that the count was not his

normal self.

"Why don't you give it a couple more weeks?" he asked. "At least until this whole Ebenezer Krim thing dies down a little."

Count Vania turned to look at Andrew, who had started hammering in the shelves again. Before he could answer him, Andrew hit the end of his finger with a hammer, causing it to bleed.

"Aaarrgh!" Andrew screamed as blood oozed in under his fingernail.

"Are you all right?" asked the count.

"Yes, I'm fine," replied Andrew. "I just hit it with the hammer, that's all."

"Well if you're okay, I'll be on my way," said the count as he turned and made his way out the door.

It wasn't until after he'd left that Andrew realized the count didn't faint like he normally does when he saw blood.

It must just be because he's preoccupied at the moment, he thought. He doesn't seem to be his normal self right now.

Outside the door, Count Vania hovered for a few seconds, then almost instantly he was gone and standing in his place was the evil gravedigger. It wasn't Count Vania at all, it was the gravedigger pretending to be him, which was why Count Vania didn't faint when he saw blood.

The gravedigger looked back through the door at Andrew. One day soon, he thought, I'll get rid of you one way or another.

Jamie stood at the school gates waiting for Paula, like he did every day. It wasn't that Paula's classes ended later than Jamie's, she just talked to her friends for much longer.

Jamie didn't say much the entire walk home. He was too busy thinking about what happened earlier in his biology class with Ebenezer Krim. But Paula always knew when something was bothering him.

"What's wrong, Jamie?" she asked.

"Nothing," he replied. Paula was already quite scared of Ebenezer Krim and Jamie didn't want to make her feel worse.

"There's obviously something wrong," she said. "You've hardly said a word the whole way home and normally you don't shut up."

On any other day, Jamie would have come back at his sister with a funny remark, and there would have been a full-scale joking match, but not today.

"I said there's nothing wrong with me," he said to her.

As they reached the entrance to the graveyard, Jamie turned around and once again saw the chilling figure of Ebenezer Krim coming toward him.

"Paula, can you see Mr. Krim over there?" Jamie said, pointing in his direction.

Paula's jaw dropped with fear. "Yes," she replied with a shiver.

Now Jamie knew he wasn't losing his mind. Ebenezer started to run toward them, laughing and screaming to frighten them.

"Run, Paula," yelled Jamie as he grabbed her arm and began to sprint down the hill to the graveyard with Mr. Krim chasing them.

"Dad, help!" Paula was screaming as they made it to the back gate.

Andrew came running from the house. "What's the matter?" he shouted as he ran toward them.

"Ebenezer Krim is chasing us!" yelled Jamie as he slammed the gate closed behind him. But just like in his biology class, as Jamie turned around, Ebenezer was gone.

"I can't see him anywhere," said Andrew. "Are you sure you saw him?"

"Yes, he was there," replied Jamie. "Ask Paula."

Both of them turned to ask Paula, but by now Paula was already inside looking back at them from the kitchen window.

"Jamie, there's no one there," added his father.

"I'm telling you, Dad, he was there," said Jamie

trying to convince him.

Andrew turned to Jamie.

"Calm down, Jamie. He's gone, there's no one there. The chances are he never was there. You probably just saw a shadow."

As Andrew put his arm around Jamie and walked him inside the house, Jamie knew there was no way he was going to convince his dad that Ebenezer Krim was chasing him. When they reached the back door, Jamie looked over his shoulder at where Ebenezer Krim had been.

There was no one there.

CHAPTER NINE

Strange Breakfast

The sizzle and smell of sausages and veggie burgers filled the kitchen. This morning, it was Jamie's turn to cook breakfast, and one by one, his guests began to arrive.

First was his father. No one liked a home-cooked breakfast more than his father.

"Mmmm," he said as he took his seat at the table. "Smells great, Jamie."

Paula walked in at the same time as Lex Killon.

"Good morning, Lex," she said as she breezed past him into the kitchen. Lex tried to answer her but as usual only succeeded in spitting salt water onto the floor.

"Has anyone seen that horrible Ebenezer Krim chap recently?" asked Lex, as he pulled out his chair.

"Jamie thinks he saw him a couple of times yesterday," Andrew replied.

"I did see him," said Jamie, still turning the sausages in the frying pan.

"You saw who?" asked Mummy as he glided through the back door and onto his chair.

"Ebenezer Krim," Paula answered.

"Oh, I wouldn't mind if I never saw him for another 2,000 years," Mummy muttered through his bandages.

Count Vania joined them in the kitchen.

"Breakfast smells good this morning, Jamie," he said before taking his seat at the table.

"It'll be ready in a few minutes," replied Jamie.

"We were chased home from school yesterday by Ebenezer Krim," Paula announced to the table.

"What?" replied Count Vania. "He chased you home?"

"Now, Paula, we discussed this last night. We don't know for sure if it was Ebenezer Krim that you saw following you," said her father.

"It was him," said Jamie adamantly.

Last to join the breakfast group was Wolfie. He slipped in quietly and sat down at the table without saying anything, which was unusual for him, because he normally had a lot to say, even first thing in the morning.

Jamie walked toward the table with a plate that was piled high with rolls, sausages, and veggie burgers, made specially for Wolfie.

"Dig in, everyone," said Jamie as he placed the plate in the middle of the table.

"What's wrong, Wolfie? You look a bit down," said Lex Killon.

"I'm just a little fed up," replied Wolfie.

"With what?" asked Andrew.

"With everything," he said, "this new house, Ebenezer Krim trying to catch us, with everything."

"Don't let it get you down, Wolfie," said Count Vania. "You'll get used to it eventually."

Andrew looked confused. Yesterday he had this same conversation with Count Vania, and now he was acting totally different.

"You've really changed your mind," said Andrew to the count.

Now the count looked confused.

"What do you mean?" asked the count.

"Well, I thought you wanted to move somewhere else, like Wolfie?"

The count looked at Andrew.

"When did I say that?" he asked, looking even more confused.

"Can I have one of those sausages, please?" shouted Wolfie, far louder than he needed to shout. It was as though he was trying to change the subject, like he had something to hide.

"Of course you can," Paula replied. "You don't need to ask, you know that."

Jamie looked at Wolfie suspiciously. He knew that something was wrong, but he couldn't put his finger on it.

Wolfie stretched out and lifted a sausage off the plate from Paula. Without thinking, he bit into it and began chewing.

"Wolfie!" Mummy yelled.

"What?" he replied.

"That's a sausage you're eating!"

"So what?" asked Wolfie.

"So it's not a veggie burger," replied Mummy, "and you're a vegetarian!"

Wolfie looked around the table at everyone, and everyone looked back at Wolfie.

Jamie knew that something didn't add up, but before he could question it, Wolfie got up from the table and ran screaming out of the door yelling, "I think I'm going be sick."

Everyone except Jamie laughed at Wolfie's mistake.

"Something's going on here," he said to the others at the table.

"Yeah," replied Paula, laughing. "He just ate half a sausage, and now he's feeling sick!"

When Wolfie returned, it seemed like he was a different Wolfie. To Jamie it was obvious he wasn't the same one that ran out the door. This Wolfie looked fine and a little taken aback with all the attention he was getting.

"Are you all right now?" asked Andrew.

"I'm fine, thank you," answered Wolfie, looking confused.

"Are you still feeling sick?" Lex Killon asked.

"Sick?" asked Wolfie. "Why would I be feeling sick?"

"Oh no," said Paula. "He's so upset that he's forgetting things now."

The others laughed. Even Wolfie laughed, although he wasn't sure what he was laughing at, he laughed anyway.

Outside, Ebenezer Krim stood watching the house again. The gravedigger appeared beside him, looking like Wolfie. It wasn't Wolfie that had taken a bite out of the sausage, it was the gravedigger pretending to be Wolfie.

"I think we need to take more drastic action," said the gravedigger in a deep, menacing voice. "They're becoming suspicious now, and I want them out of that house by tonight."

Ebenezer Krim didn't say anything, he just turned and stared back at the house, an evil grin slowly spreading across his face. It wasn't long until he was laughing out loud.

CHAPTER TEN

Unexpected Help

The lightning cracked through the window in Paula's bedroom, forcing her to pull the covers up to just below her chin. Just like the first night they arrived, there was another power outage. This time, however, everyone was too tired to play hide-and-seek and instead decided to go to bed early.

Paula didn't want to say anything to Jamie earlier as they climbed the staircase on their way to bed, but she had a horrible feeling that something bad was going to happen tonight.

Maybe if she had said something, Jamie would have told her that he had the same feeling. Now she was just counting the seconds between each bolt of lightning and roar of thunder.

Paula wasn't happy in her new house, but she was still trying to make the best of it for her dad and so was Jamie. As she turned her head to the side, with every bolt of lightning, she could see the rain running down the windowpane in long, thin streams. Her eyes felt heavy, and she started to doze off.

It wasn't so much a bang that woke her up, more that something had moved at the bottom of her bed. As she slowly opened her eyes, she felt it again.

The bottom of Paula's bed was lifting up and dropping back down onto the carpet. As she sat up, the front of her bed started to lift higher and higher and drop faster and faster.

Then suddenly it just stopped.

I know, thought Paula, it must be Wolfie or Mummy underneath my bed trying to scare me.

Paula slowly crept to the bottom of her bed on her hands and knees, and as quick as she could, she pulled up her bedsheets and stuck her head under the bed.

"Gotcha!" she yelled, expecting to see one of her ghost friends, but there was no one under her bed.

Where could they have gone, she thought as she sat back up. Then she felt it again.

This time the bed lifted high off the ground and dropped back onto the floor with a heavy thud. Now Paula was really starting to get scared. If it's a ghost, why can't I see it?

"Who's there?" she yelled out across her room, but there was silence.

At first, Paula was so busy listening for noises that she didn't realize the front of her bed was slowly lifting again. Then it dropped, straight onto the floor with a loud crash and lifted again and dropped again and lifted and dropped and lifted and dropped.

Paula was screaming.

"Dad! Jamie! Help me!" she yelled over and over again, until her door was kicked open. Instantly her bed fell to the floor.

Her dad was standing in the doorway with Jamie behind him.

"What's wrong, Paula?" he shouted as they raced to her bed.

"There's something under my bed, Dad, and I don't know what it is and I can't see it," she said.

Jamie looked under her bed and saw nothing there.

"There's nothing under your bed, Paula," he said to his little sister.

Andrew held Paula in his arms. "You had a bad dream Paula, that's all," he said. "Everyone has bad dreams."

"This wasn't a bad dream, Dad," she said. "It was real. The bed was lifting up and dropping really fast."

Her father looked into her tearful eyes and said, "It wasn't real, Paula. It just felt real, that's all."

Jamie looked under the bed again. Without raising his head, he said to his father, "Dad, I think you should see this."

Jamie's dad climbed down beside Jamie and peered under the bed. Jamie pointed to the marks on Paula's carpet that the leg on the bottom of her bed had made, and there were lots of marks. Paula's bed had obviously been moved.

"Paula, I don't want you to panic," said her dad, "but get out of your bed slowly and stand behind me."

Jamie and his dad stood up and slowly made their way to the door with Paula. It was still dark in the room and very difficult to see where they were going. Every time there was a bolt of lightning, it allowed Jamie to see the whole room light up for a split second. As Jamie turned to see his father and sister, a bolt of lightning lit up something that was floating on the other end of the room.

Jamie couldn't see what it was, but he knew it was getting closer and closer.

"Look out, Jamie!" yelled his father, as he pushed

Jamie out of the way.

As Jamie fell, he heard a smash, and his father landed on top of him. He could see he had been knocked unconscious by a vase.

Paula stood in the middle of the floor screaming at the top of her lungs. All around her things were falling off the walls—pictures, ornaments, and toys.

"Jamie, help me!" she yelled.

"I can't, Paula. I'm trapped. Dad's on my legs and I can't get them free," he shouted back.

In the middle of the havoc, Jamie was thankful to see Lex Killon.

"I'll help you, Jamie!" he screamed, as he tried to push Jamie's dad off his legs.

Behind Jamie, Paula's bedroom door was kicked open, and in the doorway stood Ebenezer Krim with his machine strapped to him.

"Leave us alone!" yelled Jamie.

He looked down at Jamie and Lex Killon on the floor, and then over to Paula, who was crying in the middle of the room.

"No one was supposed to get hurt, gravedigger," screamed Ebenezer over the noise.

"Get out of here, Krim," roared a deep voice from the darkness of Paula's room, and the bedroom door slammed closed again.

Jamie could see Ebenezer Krim had his foot jammed in the door. He took off his machine, switched it on, and threw it to Jamie.

"Jamie, use this," he shouted.

"What do I do?" asked Jamie.

"Just pick it up, flip the switch, and point it at the gravedigger."

Jamie stretched out his hand. He could barely reach the machine and had to push his father off his legs a little more before he finally managed to grab it. As he spun around with the machine, he could see two Lex Killons side by side.

The one on the left shouted, "Jamie, kill the other one. I'm the real Lex."

"No, Jamie," the one on the right shouted. "I'm the real Lex."

Paula was still screaming in the middle of the floor. Jamie looked at one Lex and then the other and couldn't tell them apart.

"Do it, Jamie! Kill him now!" screamed the Lex on the left. Jamie spun the machine around to the other one.

"I don't know which one is which!" Jamie shouted to Mr. Krim.

"Well suck them both up," he shouted.

As Jamie prepared to turn the machine on, the Lex on the right tried to say something. As a bolt of lightning lit up the room, Jamie saw him spit out some salt water.

"That's good enough for me!" he shouted, flipped the switch, and pointed it at the one on the left, sucking him inside instantly before he could try and get away.

"Turn the machine off!" yelled the real Lex

Killon, who was holding on to Paula's wardrobe to stop himself being sucked inside.

Jamie turned it off, and the room fell silent. Paula stopped screaming, and their father began to wake up.

Jamie turned to Ebenezer Krim and said something he never thought he would ever say, "Thank you."

CHAPTER ELEVEN

Here We Go Again

"That's the last of it," said Andrew as he strapped the final box to the roof of the car. Jamie and Paula were glad. Even though the gravedigger was gone, everyone was still relieved that they didn't have to live in that house anymore—even the ghosts were relieved.

As a way of saying thank you to Ebenezer Krim for helping to save their lives, Andrew agreed to sell him their house in the graveyard.

As the car rolled out of the driveway for the last time with Jamie, Andrew, and Paula inside, Jamie looked back over his shoulder to the house that was his home for such a short time. He wasn't sad he was leaving. He just wanted to have one last look.

Ebenezer Krim stood at the gate, watching them leave, even though he now owned the house he'd always wanted, he still wouldn't smile. He just stood at the gate, staring after them.

"So, Dad, about this new house," said Paula, "where exactly is it?"

"It's about a two-mile drive from here," replied her father, "and it's a surprise."

"Can't you tell us any more than that?" Jamie asked him.

"I'll tell you one thing," he said. "Your new house used to be an old church."

"An old church!" yelled Jamie and Paula together.

"Have you lost your mind?" asked Jamie.

His father just laughed, glancing at them in the rearview mirror. He gave them that silly smile, winked, and said, "Aw come on kids...trust me."

Jamie and Paula looked at each other in disbelief.

"Oh no," said Paula. "Here we go again."

Read on to enjoy an excerpt from another
haunting title in the Creepers series:

Pen Pals

by Edgar J. Hyde

Illustrations by Chloe Tyler

CHAPTER ONE

The Note

"Natasha Morris, will you please tell me, and the rest of your classmates, what on earth is so interesting outside?"

With a jolt, Natasha turned toward the teacher.

"I'm sorry, Miss Harrison, I was just thinking about..." Natasha's voice trailed off.

She couldn't think of an excuse, and she couldn't possibly tell the truth—that this morning's long-winded history lesson was boring! After all, wasn't history supposed to be about Henry VIII and his six wives, romance, divorce, and gory beheadings? Instead she was having to sit and listen for two hours about crop rotation! Crop rotation—who cares?

"No. Don't even bother stuttering your way through an excuse, just do me a favor and pay attention. Remember you have a test coming up next week, and crop rotation just might be one of the questions!" Miss Harrison turned to the rest of the class. "Now, where were we?" Her voice droned on and on.

Olivia turned and smiled at Natasha sympathetically. The two were best friends and had been since they first met up as four-year-olds in the same preschool. They were now in their first year of high school, enjoying feeling grown-up, carrying their books from class to class around the massive, never-ending hallways, giggling as they frequently got lost, only to arrive red and breathless to their next class. They had made new friends, too.

There was Ellis, with her dark curly hair and large brown eyes. Natasha envied her. Then there was Marcie, though Natasha couldn't make up her mind about her just yet. She was the complete opposite of Ellis, pale with long, straw-like blonde hair and somewhat on the quiet side. Pale and interesting, I guess, if you were being nice, thought Natasha.

She hastily scribbled a note and passed it to Olivia without Miss Harrison noticing.

Meet you outside the library at four.

Olivia quickly pushed the note inside her notebook and gave no sign of having received anything.

Natasha looked at her watch. Ten minutes past four. Where on earth was Olivia? Just then, she saw Olivia, Marcie, and Ellis wind their way up the long path from the front of the school.

"You took your time." She smiled as all three girls stopped just beside her.

"Sorry, Natasha, it's my fault," said Ellis. "I left my new favorite lip gloss in the bathroom and had to go get it. You never know who you might see on the way home."

Ellis was always experimenting with lip gloss and eye shadow and always on the lookout for free samples. She would come to school drenched in perfume, having spent the weekend in the perfume department of the nearest store.

"You should try some, Marcie. Look, it's a pale pink, it'd look great on you."

"Gosh, no," said Marcie. "My mom would freak out. She says there's plenty of time to put all that 'junk,' as she calls it, on my face. Anyway, I'd rather keep my money for important things. I'm going to buy some new headphones this weekend, at least they will last longer than your makeup will!"

"Hey, Ellis," someone shouted from behind them. The girls turned to see Scott Gregson across from them. He was the best looking guy in their grade, and everyone had their eye on him. "If you're going home, I'll walk with you."

Ellis smiled. "See what the 'junk' on your face does for you, girls," she muttered. "Sure, Scott, I was just saying goodbye to the girls. See you tomorrow, everybody." And off she went, pink lips glistening, dark curls bouncing, backpack slung casually over her arm.

"Don't you just wish you had her confidence," sighed Olivia.

"Yes, and her hair and her teeth and her eyes," replied Natasha. "Never mind, 'Make the best of what you've got' is what my mom always says. Now let's see, what could you make out of the three of us?"

And as the three started to make their way home, they laughed together, picking out the parts of each other that they thought were the "best."

"Okay, Natasha," said Olivia, "you give me your tiny waist, Marcie can give me her small perfectly shaped feet, and I can probably get away with using my own hands—if I paint my fingernails—and with the help of a wig, there we have it, the perfect girl!"

And so the conversation carried on until the girls were almost home.

"Oh, and Natasha," Olivia began, "next time you write me a note in class, you really don't have to write my full name on it. I know who I am!"

Natasha looked at Olivia. "I didn't write your full name, Olivia. In fact, I didn't even write your first name!"

"Yes, you did," Olivia laughed, as she fished in both jacket pockets for the note. "You wrote, 'Olivia Goulden, meet you outside the library at four.' Darn, I can't find the note—oh, look, here it is."

They had now reached Marcie's house and Olivia had emptied the contents of her backpack onto the pavement outside. She showed the hastily scrawled note to Natasha and sure enough, Olivia's name was written above what Natasha remembered writing.

Olivia Goulden,
Meet you outside the library at four.

"That's really weird, Olivia. I don't remember writing that, it doesn't even look like my handwriting."

"Marcie, where have you been?" the girls heard Marcie's mom shout from an upstairs window.

"Oops, gotta go! Mom wants me to go to the grocery store with her today. See you tomorrow."

"Bye, Marcie," called the two girls as she disappeared inside her front door.

Natasha was still staring at the note.

"Stop trying to be funny, Natasha. I mean if you passed the note straight to me and I didn't add my own name to it, then who did?" Olivia protested. "Anyway, look, I have to run too. I'm babysitting Mrs. Winter's twins tonight, and I have to try and get my homework done before I go. I'll see you tomorrow."

"All right," sighed Natasha, "but I still don't understand."

She left Olivia at the end of the street where the road leading to her house forked left.

Weird, she thought as she walked, she must have been in more of a bored stupor than she realized this morning. How could you write someone's name and not remember?

"Suzanna Craigson," she read aloud from one of the gravestones in the cemetery. She had to pass the cemetery every morning and afternoon going to and from school, and although she was never comfortable with it, she found the best way around it was to make up stories about the people lying beneath the rows and rows of tombstones. That way it took the scariness out of it.

"Born November 2, 1806. Cruelly taken from her beloved parents November 1, 1820."

Natasha had never noticed that particular stone before, or maybe it was just that she had never

actually realized how young Suzanna had been when she died.

Wonder what happened to her, she thought. The use of the word "cruelly" seemed to indicate murder or something gory and horrible.

Better stop thinking about it, she decided. Mom always says my imagination's too vivid. It'll end up getting me into trouble one of these days.

"Here comes fatso, here comes fatso." Her young brother's chanting soon stopped her daydreaming.

"Come here, Tommy, you little brat," she laughed, chasing the bubbly little three-year-old into the backyard. "I'll show you fatso."

She grabbed him and hugged him tightly around the waist, lifting him right off his feet. She kissed him loudly on the lips and came away covered in green sticky goo.

"What have you been eating now?" She smiled.

"Gooey monsters," he said and showed her the

empty packet in his tiny hand.

"Green Slimy Guts," she read aloud. "Made from jelly and packets of sugar and full of additives." She added, "Your teeth will fall out," and poked him in the tummy playfully.

"Don't care about teef," he retorted. "Like gooey monsters!"

How did the rhyme go, she mused as she went inside to change. Sugar and spice and all things nice, oh yes, frogs and snails and puppy dogs' tails, or something like that. Tommy was that, all right, and she adored every last little inch of him. She wondered if Suzanna Craigson had had a brother.

CHAPTER TWO

Look Out!

The next morning, Natasha simply couldn't believe they were having to play soccer outside in the rain. It had started to rain last night and hadn't let up from then until now, so the field was virtually flooded! Their gym teacher, however, had insisted that they change and "get on out there! Rain never hurt anyone!" So there they were, trying desperately to run around, but usually ending up sprawled on the ground with the ball and legs flying every way but the right way!

Natasha walked over to where Olivia was standing near the goal. Both Olivia and Marcie hated sports of any kind and were both trying to look small and insignificant so that Miss Starrs wouldn't notice they weren't participating in the game.

"Managing to get away with it so far?" she hissed at the pair.

Olivia raised her eyes up. "I'm so wet and dirty, I'll have to soak in a hot bubble bath for at least three hours tonight!"

Natasha laughed. Just then, one of the girls at the far end of the field started to run toward them. As she drew nearer, Natasha realized that the girl was Ellis, wearing a brand new bright orange and green headband. Ellis drew her foot back and kicked the ball as hard as she could.

The ball seemed to be heading straight for Olivia. Natasha moved forward to try and stop it, but to her surprise, Marcie moved out in front of her. She took a swipe at the ball, but misjudging the wet ground, leaned too far forward, causing herself to skid in the mud. She slid far down the field, turning around to face the opposite direction. The ball flew through the air. Natasha grabbed Olivia.

"Olivia, look out!" she shouted as both girls fell to the ground waiting for the sickening thud.

The ball landed just beside Natasha's right foot, narrowly missing hitting either of the girls, on almost the exact spot where Olivia had been standing a few short seconds before.

Miss Starrs was running down the field, wet hair standing straight up, eyes wide with horror, unsure whether or not anyone had been hurt.

"Natasha, Olivia, are you all right? Oh, thank goodness!" she said as both girls stood up. Both their faces were streaked with mud, their gym shorts and T-shirts dirty and soaked. "Go inside and take a hot shower, girls," she said gently, "while I attend to Marcie."

Marcie too was on her feet. "I'm sorry, Olivia, Miss Starrs, I was only trying to block..." She was crying now, her pale cheeks even paler than normal.

"Go inside, Marcie," said Miss Starrs. "Go ahead, follow the girls in and take a hot shower. I'll come and see you all in a minute or two."

Miss Starrs gently herded the girls into the school then went back to the top of the field. She checked her watch—only about ten minutes to go. She'd let the three girls have some time to themselves and then get the rest of the class inside and cleaned up. She blew the whistle for the girls to play on and heaved a sigh of relief. She'd thought her recently completed first aid course was finally going to come in handy! She looked around to see where Ellis went; Miss Starrs knew she hadn't meant any harm, but since she was the one who kicked the offending ball, she was sure she'd be concerned about Olivia.

She finally spotted her, standing on her own on one side of the field. Now isn't that strange. Miss Starrs shook her head. She had thought Olivia and Ellis were friends. Maybe she was wrong. She tried to shake some of the rain from her hair and ran up the field to make sure nothing else was going on.

Ellis admired her new tennis shoes. She thought the green flash on the side matched her new headband really well.

☁ ☁ ☁

Marcie was drying off after her warm shower. The girl was shaking from the shock of what had almost happened.

"I really am sorry, Olivia," she kept repeating. "I was only trying to block the shot. I could see from where I was standing that Ellis was going to make a direct hit. I mean, I don't mean that she meant to hit you, just that I could see that it looked like...Oh, I don't know what I mean anymore. I really am so sorry," she finished.

Olivia put her arms around the tearful girl.

"Look, Marcie, I really appreciate what you did out there just now. But the truth is that no harm was done and I'm eternally grateful to you for getting me off that cold, wet field and into this warm shower, so no more tears, okay?"

Marcie smiled. "Okay, if you're sure you forgive me."

"And, hey," joked Natasha, "aren't you a dark horse? I thought you hated soccer, yet there you were, diving in front of people, going after balls— quite the little athletic heroine. Just shows what friends will do for you. You're lucky, Olivia," she finished.

Marcie looked apprehensive but when she realized that Natasha was genuinely congratulating her, she visibly relaxed.

"Let's get dressed and get out of here," said Olivia, "before the rest of the class comes in and we're caught up in the stampede. And remember we have to pick up our class photos today. I can't wait to see how awful we look and who has the worst acne!"

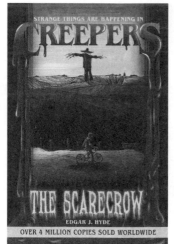

tles in the Creepers series!

The Piano
ISBN: 9781486718764

Cold Kisser
ISBN: 9781486718740

The Gravedigger
ISBN: 9781486718795

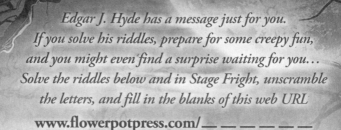

Edgar J. Hyde has a message just for you.
If you solve his riddles, prepare for some creepy fun,
and you might even find a surprise waiting for you...
Solve the riddles below and in Stage Fright, unscramble
the letters, and fill in the blanks of this web URL

www.flowerpotpress.com/ _ _ _ _ _ _ _

with the answers you find. Go to the website
with your parent's permission and find out
what waits on the other side.

1. A simple game of Leap Frog gone horribly wrong. Gravestones toppled over with reckless abandon. How many gravestones were knocked over? Go to the page with that number, hop down to the fifth paragraph, and leap over to the 22nd word. What letter does it start with?

2. A group of creepy monsters are this family's lifelong friends. One of these monsters has cousins who live at the museum. What letter does this character's name start with?

3. No matter where this family moves, ghoulish spirits are sure to follow. Especially when they move to a cemetery! What letter does the family's last name in this story start with?